# THE BARITONE CAT

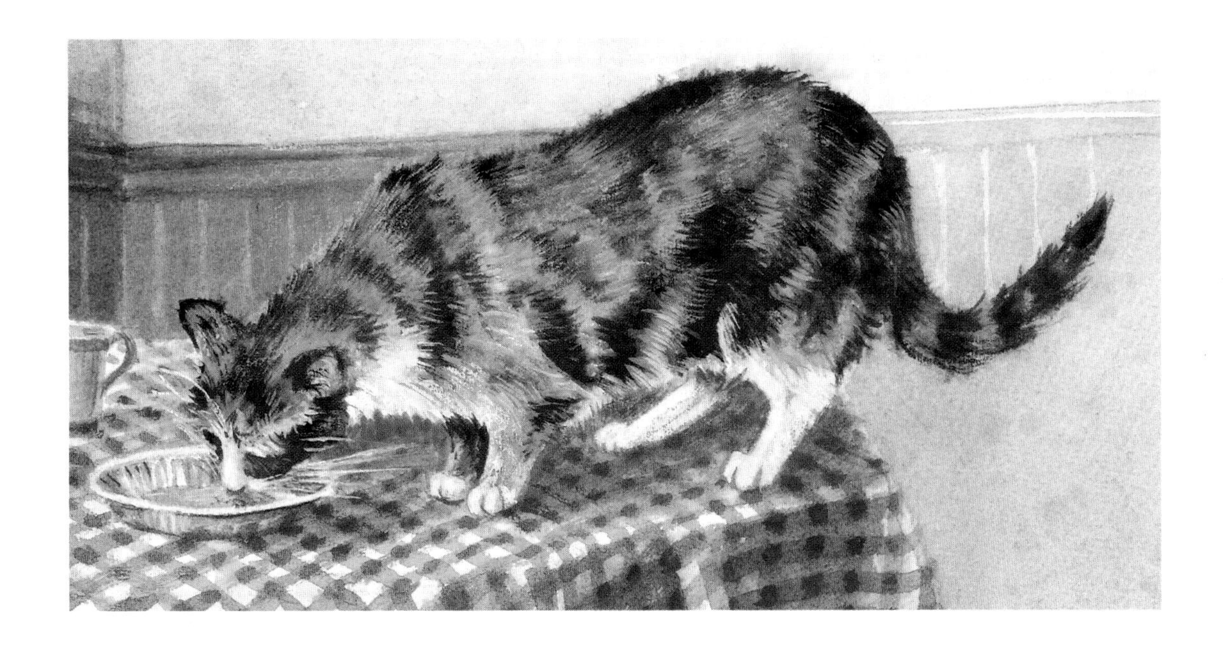

MORA SKELTON

ILLUSTRATED BY JANET WILSON

LESTER PUBLISHING LIMITED

 Lester Publishing Limited acknowledges the financial assistance of the Canada Council and the Ontario Arts Council.

---

CANADIAN CATALOGUING IN PUBLICATION DATA

Skelton, Mora
The baritone cat
ISBN 1-895555-52-3
1. Cats - Juvenile fiction. I. Wilson, Janet, 1952- . II. Title.
PS8587.K45B3 1994 jC813'.54 C93-095160-3
PZ7.S54Ba 1994

---

Lester Publishing Limited
56 The Esplanade
Toronto, Ontario
Canada M5E 1A7

Printed and bound in Hong Kong

94 95 96 97 5 4 3 2 1

*To my sister, Eleanor, and to Sam himself*

M. S.

*To my friend and teacher, James Hill*

J. W.

Sam was a cat who loved three things. He loved to roam, he loved to eat, and he loved to sing. On a crisp autumn night he sang with the neighborhood cats in the backyards of Cheshire Court. In his big, warm voice Sam sang his song:

*I want to be free, purr-fect-ly free,*
*Like a bird, or a bee,*
*Or a bold chimpanzee.*
*No locked doors for me —*
*I'M SAM!*

In the cold dawn the members of the choir crept to their homes — all except Sam. He had no home.

Hunger tightened his stomach. Sam thought about the things he would like to eat.

Mice were his first choice, but most of them lived inside those huge brick houses where Sam couldn't get at them. "Humans guard them like treasures," he grumbled.

Birds came next on the list. “But it’s fall now,” thought Sam, “and even the robins are getting scarce.” He licked his lips. Most young birds, once so easy to catch, had grown up and were flying south.

Then he thought about leftovers. These were usually served in large, green garbage bags. Each bag was a puzzle. He would try to find a sweet-smelling anchovy or a scrap of salami among all those potato peels.

Sam's food dream was interrupted by the voice of his best friend. "Come home with me and we'll see if my folks will give you dinner," said Henry.

On the way, Sam stopped dead in front of a broken-down house. "That used to be my home," he said, ears drooping.

Sam could not remember the time before he went to live with Mr. Saunders. He thought the old gentleman was perfect. They only met at meals. "We ate together at the same table," Sam explained to Henry, "from two shiny pie plates." Sam had a song for Mr. Saunders:

*We're a rough bunch of cats where I'm from,*
*And I'm rougher and tougher than some.*
*I want to be free, I want to be me.*
*That's why, when you call, I don't come —*
*I'M SAM!*

But one day Mr. Saunders got sick. His daughter came to live with him, and she hated cats. She locked the screen door, the one Sam used to open by himself.

Sam had no home anymore. He shivered and turned to follow Henry.

When the two cats finally arrived at Henry's house, Mrs. Clark opened the door just long enough to let her own cat come in. "But not *you*," she said firmly, closing the door on Sam.

He stood outside, wondering what to do next.

"I'll have to steal," Sam said to himself. "I'll have to grab some other animal's dinner before he gets it."

He thought of Wilbur, an English sheepdog who spent most of his time at the end of a long rope. Wilbur's food bowl stood just outside the door of his doghouse.

Crouching in the bushes, Sam waited for his chance. He crept down to Wilbur's dish, but two mouthfuls later was fleeing for his life.

"Come back here!" roared Wilbur. But he was checked by his rope just short of Sam's tail.

Then Sam thought of Dee Dee and Mingo. They were fed in their house, but an open basement window let them run outside whenever they pleased. If they could get out, then Sam could get in to look for food.

At the window Sam cocked his head. No sound of human activity came from within. Reckless with hunger, he squeezed inside.

Sam sped up the basement steps into the kitchen. He found several plates filled with food, just waiting to be sampled. Sam lapped up a dish of milk as fast as he could. Each sip tasted perfect.

"Stop that," a voice demanded. It was Dee Dee. "That's my dinner you're eating. Mine and Mingo's."

"Too bad," said Sam, his mouth full. Gobbling hard, he moved like a vacuum cleaner over the dishes.

"Thief! Flea bag! Nogoodnick!" Dee Dee screeched.

"You should be ashamed," scolded a new, dignified voice. Mingo had entered the room. "We'll tell Joanne on you. She takes care of us."

Sam didn't care. Mean from lack of food, he flattened his ears and glared at them, but he didn't retreat until he had finished every morsel. Then, his eyes narrow and dangerous, Sam backed toward the basement stairs.

The next morning Sam arrived at Dee Dee and Mingo's house again. He scrambled through the window, up the basement stairs . . . and found a lady in the kitchen.

"Out you go, you bold thing," she exclaimed, pushing him with the broom.

Dee Dee and Mingo stared at Sam, safe behind her legs.

"Stop, Mom! Isn't this Sam, Mr. Saunders' cat?" asked a little girl. She spoke gently and reached out to pick him up.

Quick as a snake, Sam whirled around and bit her. Then he was gone, down the basement steps.

"Did he break the skin, Joanne?" cried her mother.

"No. I guess he's just not used to being with people." Joanne buried her face in Mingo's soft fur and thought about poor Sam all alone in the cold.

The chill of winter was in the air when Sam returned to Dee Dee and Mingo's house the next day. The wind ruffled his fur and stirred the dry leaves. The bellowing TV and laughter inside the house told him that the family was home. He couldn't go in.

Sam lay down. He felt strangely tired and low in spirits. He waited — cold, forlorn, unwelcome.

Suddenly, he sensed he was no longer alone. He turned and recognized Joanne. Sam was about to fade into the bushes, but he held back. "Maybe it's time I stopped running."

"Would you like to give me something to eat or drink?" he meowed. "Would you like to adopt me?" It was a dignified inquiry.

Joanne saw the ruffled fur, the large head on the painfully thin body, an unhealed wound from a long-ago fight. She picked him up gingerly, wary of his teeth, but this time Sam was prepared.

"Don't bite. Don't wriggle. Don't stick your claws into her," he commanded himself. "Give it a chance to work." And off he floated into the house, wrapped in Joanne's arms.

Weeks passed. Frigid air gusted between the brick houses, the ground grew hard and snow swirled down from the gray skies. But the house was warm and good. Dee Dee and Mingo hadn't welcomed Sam at first, but they couldn't resist the songs he sang to them in his deep, beautiful voice. Soon they were glad to see him and he grew equally fond of them. And of Joanne too.

When Sam sat up tall on the front steps of 45 Cheshire Court, he was a big, husky cat who would make any family proud.

One day a new song began inside Sam. It started as a quiet purr, but when he opened his mouth, the song poured out in his fine, baritone voice:

*I've got a family and a warm place to call home,*
*I've got new friends and that's more than some.*
*I still want to be free, I still want to be me,*
*But now, when you call, I might come —*
*I'M SAM!*